BOOK ONE
OF
THE PISS MAP
SERIES

*Also by Louie Crowder*

*A Better House for Ritchie* (PLAY)

*In Irons* (PRINT & E-BOOK)

# HENRY GEREIGHTY

### A NOVEL

### BY

## LOUIE CROWDER

NEXT LEFT PRESS
ASCENSION, LA

**Henry Gereighty**
Copyright © 2015 by Louie Crowder

Published in the United States of America by
Next Left Press
Ascension Parish, LA 70734
www.nextleftpress.com

Layout and Cover Design by Geoff Munsterman

ISBN: 978-0-9962374-1-3

*For Maya Deren*
*For Gina Vega*
*For Otter, and for Chris (aka Bacchus)*
*And with my undying gratitude to Larry Kramer.*

# Henry Gereighty

# 1

FROM his earliest memories, Henry Gereighty knew
the human heart was a metronome. He knew that to write
was to paint was to sing was to dance was to laugh, that all
those things were manifestations of the rhythms of the human heart and the heart, being an expression of the magic
of God, kept time to life. He lived his adolescence with the
spirited romp of a cartoon. On any typical day he would
draw pictures, then run with them through the house
to find anyone he could. He would corner Anyone while
describing his pictures in excruciating detail, elaborately
explaining the interior dialogues between stick figures and
their God. When finished with that he would wrap up the
performance with an interpretive dance. Mostly his creative
work would be received by reviews: "It's a good thing our
great grandparents came down from the mountain when
they did;" "This family needs fresh blood;" and, "People are
starting to get goofy."

Henry maintained his eccentric labeling until puberty. It
was the onset of puberty, when Henry discovered his natural
attractions, that he was re-categorized from Eccentric to
Sick. Being Spiritually Corrupt in the eyes of those whom
he loved shut him down.

Living in isolation, surrounded by people who hated all
he was becoming, he stopped drawing and began to write.
He not only found writing to be more satisfying, it was

easier to hide. For ten years Henry read and wrote in captivity. He read to feel good and he wrote to rid himself of hatred.

In the 1980s the President of the United States committed an act of Genocide against the gay community, declaring war not only on a generation of men given a death sentence, but on an entire generation of children discovering who they were. Henry was taught to hate himself; existing in Survivor Mode, navigating a violent Christian occupation that kept him isolated and in fear of all the things he was. *There's something wrong with me*, he would confide to no one with his head in his hands, tears falling from his eyes onto the tops of his tanned southern feet.

Truthfully Henry Gereighty missed his life's calling. He was meant to be a preacher. Even a stargazer with rudimentary abilities could have seen that imprint in the Heavens. More likely than not had the Blue Ridge world that he loved loved him in return he would have never left the mountains. He would be a pastor somewhere along the Mystical Highway that connects Asheville, North Carolina and Johnson City, Tennessee. But his Southern Appalachian world did not love him so he took his love and left.

He fled the mountains to New Orleans because Tennessee Williams had gone to New Orleans. Tennessee saved more Southern gay men than he could ever know by simply telling them they were not alone.

The City of New Orleans taught Henry Gereighty how to be gay. Then, despite the Southern world that questioned his existence, he taught himself how to be a playwright.

# 2

BEFORE The Catastrophe there were two Gay Americas: Progressive, and Traditional. The Progressive Gay America consisted of the coasts and enclaves. The other one was the conservative Midwest and the South: two sets of civil rights, two interpretations of reasonable freedoms. New Orleans had historically existed outside American culture, and being detached from national cultural norms, stood separate from the extremes as a safe haven, an island of sorts.

After The Catastrophe there were still two Gay Americas, but the island of New Orleans was no more. The population shift flooded the city with Midwestern and Northern Hatreds. The enclave became the French Quarter, and as the transformation from New Orleans to The City of NO progressed, the enclave became a small section of the French Quarter labeled The Fruit Loop.

The Southern Liberal Elite replaced New Orleans with The City of NO. Because Henry's entire life had happened in Survival Mode he was able to sustain himself during the terrible early years that followed The Catastrophe. He, and artists like him, kept the candles lit even into the darkest days. He was one of the few playwrights left on the Gulf Coast: most of the artists killed themselves, or evacuated to never return. Although The Catastrophe had untethered the Survivors to any secure mooring, they operated regardless, adrift in the violent minefield the city had become.

Henry spent the first two years after The Storm in a flurry of reading and writing. The reading gave him escape, but the writing didn't release the anger. He became a pain junkie. By some sort of miracle he was not an alcoholic, nor did he shoot-up. He fought, badly. Most of the brawls were simple: a verbal altercation followed by a brief fistfight. Sometimes, at the beginning, Henry would get a solid blow in by throwing the first punch. Mostly, he took punches.

In the Spring of 2008, Henry groped a National Guardsman. It seemed reasonable at the time. He had been slamming car bombs at My Enemy's Dog on Lower Decatur Street. The plan was to catch a quick, hard buzz before heading home. When the quick hard buzz came it was followed by a duo of Guardsmen making their rounds, as The City of NO was still under Marshall Law.

"Our salvation," Henry said to the soldiers.

They both smiled and walked past.

Henry followed them. "Where are you guys from?"

"Indiana," the younger of the two said.

"I'll buy the both of you a drink," he said then turned to the bar. "Two Guinness for our Salvateur from Indiana."

"We can't but thank you," the younger of the two said.

"You're welcome," Henry said. "Politeness gets you everything; in the event you were curious."

The Guardsmen smiled and finished their walk-through and left.

Henry followed them.

The Guardsmen made their way down Decatur Street to Governor Nichols, then turned right towards the French Market.

Henry followed them. "Excuse me," he said.

The soldiers stopped.

"I know you're busy. I don't mean to bother you," he said as he extended his hand to the younger of the two.

The young soldier slipped his hand into his pocket.

"I'm Henry. I wanted to officially introduce myself to you. I realize you're probably not gay but I am and you are a very, very attractive man. So there. That's what I had to say. I'll be on my way now." He turned back towards My Enemy's Dog.

"Wait a minute," the young Guardsman said.

Henry stopped.

"Do you always think you know what everyone else is thinking?" The young Guardsman said. Then he nodded to the older soldier who stepped back.

"The only time I make that assumption is when I'm interested in someone," Henry said. "I assume whatever I need to think to soften the blow when the object of my interest is ambivalent. It seems giving us both a way out is a generous way to operate."

"What if I am interested?" The young Guardsman said.

"Then I'm the lucky one, aren't I?"

He leaned in to kiss Henry.

Henry slid a hand down the young Guardsman's side to his waist, then cupped his crotch.

In a swift, fluid motion, the older soldier took Henry down, and pinned him to the ground. He held Henry against the curb. "Which hand did he grab you with?" He asked his partner.

"The right one."

Then the older soldier took Henry's right arm and held it at a slant from the curb to the street as the younger man stomped on Henry's arm, snapping the bone in half.

The young man leaned down, rubbing his face against Henrys. He softly kissed Henry's cheek and whispered, "Ssshhh," before he kissed his lips and stood.

The older one let Henry go and the Guardsmen resumed their rounds.

# 3

HENRY Gereighty left The City of NO and bought a shotgun house in Pass Christian, Mississippi with the intentions of living a quiet life by the Gulf. *From this point on,* he told himself, *my life will be different. I will live with seriousness and intention. I'll re-read the works of Thomas Wolfe and Tennessee Williams and I'll age simply and happily by the sea.*

Having no furniture and no extra money Henry bought a package of cheap magic markers; it was a rainbow pack, all the colors he wanted to fill his life with. He opened the windows to smell the Gulf of Mexico and clean the house of the chemical stench from the markers as he drew furniture in each room. He started in the bedroom. He drew a four-poster antique bed with a canopy, Italian leather chairs, and Venetian chandeliers. There were vases from the Ming Dynasty, and priceless Egyptian artifacts. The floor was covered in hand-woven Romanian rugs, a mahogany wardrobe sat like royalty against the far wall juxtaposed with a floor to ceiling mirror that was modeled from a similar piece in the plantations along the Mississippi River by Zachary, Louisiana. He was meticulous in the details of the decorating. It made sleeping in a vacant room, on a bare mattress on naked wooden floors, damp from humidity and his own sweat, less depressing than the realities of southern poverty.

After finishing the bedroom he moved into the front room. This room had to be approached differently. It was where he worked; where he wrote and read. It was a place of action and the things he allowed inside it had to facilitate the transformations of contemplation to movement. He put a dining table in the middle of the floor with a folding metal chair, his computer, printer, and stack of books. The only other thing in the room was an antique coffin he had found in a junk shop in Long Beach. *The coffin gives the place a sense of urgency*, he thought as he dragged it in through the front door. Next he carried in a ladder and drew a map of the state of Indiana onto one of the blank walls. Then he drew a National Guard emblem in the state, and with his good hand he punched a hole into the wall.

In Pass Christian, Mississippi, like in all good Southern Gothic small towns in the Year of Our Lord 2008, there lived a gimp. He lived in a nice house on the other side of the graveyard from Henry; concealed from the rest of the world by a thicket of sweet olive trees. He would walk the railroad every morning wearing a cape. He would throw big rocks from the tracks at Henry Gereighty's house yelling, "I know what you are." He would make three passes during the day: breakfast, lunch, and dinner. The rocks would start raining onto the metal roof of Henry's house at 8 am every morning. The consistency made Henry very productive. Henry would get coffee started then spend the first three hours of the day writing. He had found the writing was best before the outside world touched his thoughts. After the writing was done he would head into the backyard to shower in the outdoor stall he had built. By the time his morning routine had finished the gimp would be making his noon-time rounds. This time Henry would yell out the side porch to the gimp, "Good day to you, Thaddeus."

"I know what you are!" the gimp would yell back.

Henry felt lucky for having achieved simplicity with his life, even with the eccentricities that accompany outcasts.

After Henry had the pins and screws removed from his arm he sat on the porch swing because the day was beautiful. The weather had not yet become too hot, a breeze came in from the Gulf, and he thought about what it meant to be happy. As he felt himself smile Thaddeus threw a dinner-time rock and caught him in the mouth. "Goddammit, Thaddeus," Henry yelled.

"I know what you are!" Thaddeus yelled back as he ran down the tracks.

Henry went inside to clean his busted lip.

He then stood in the middle of the living room staring at the other three blank walls. He grabbed one of the markers and the ladder and went to the top of the wall facing the State of Indiana and wrote: The Fuck You Wall in big red letters. Under the heading he wrote: 1. The National Guard of Indiana, and 2. Thaddeus the Rock Thrower. He climbed off the ladder, stepped back, and had a good look at it. He could feel something stirring deep inside that gave him warmth he was unfamiliar with. It was a pleasant and even exhilarating sensation and he felt confident that whatever was happening in his living room was good: The Fuck You Wall was good.

# 4

HENRY'S life in Pass Christian fell into rhythm with the Gimp Rock Alarm Clock.

Awake now every day at 8 am Henry became very productive. After a few months he finished the new play, *Chapeau Tombe Nan La Mer*, and on the front page he dedicated it to Thaddeus The Rock Thrower for his punctuality. Henry had been working on the play for a year. When a writer invests into a piece the world where they sleep and eat is sacrificed so the world they are creating can be given life; both worlds cannot exist simultaneously. One or the other has to prevail. The pro of that exchange is manifestation of an end product. The con is the obliteration of the writer's personal life. With the new manuscript in hand Henry drove over to The City of NO to meet with a gatekeeper for funding. It had taken time to arrange the meeting. Each time, returning to the world of NO had become increasingly difficult. Some of that difficulty came from broken ties, some from waning interest. The older he became the more difficult it was convincing himself of the plausibility of economic sacrifice to his form of art.

"You know, Henry, I like your writing," the gatekeeper/ producer said. "I always have. And I respect the fact that you've become this self-producing playwright over the years. I probably shouldn't say this, but I will: write a play with naked boys spouting your poetry, then I'll produce it for you. The days of community theatre are over. It's too expensive. Be practical, Henry, dear; and make it funny. *Naked Boys Singing, Part 2*. People will pay to see swinging dicks, regardless of what the storyline is - and if you make them laugh in the process they'll tell their friends to come see it, too. And that's what you want. It's what we all want, isn't it?"

When Henry got back to Pass Christian he made his third entry onto The Fuck You Wall. He stepped back, looked at it; it did not make him feel better. He punched the wall.

His wrist swelled instantaneously. He took a couple of sticks from the backyard and made a splint before going to the Emergency Room.

After getting a professional splint on his wrist he sat on the sun porch with a bottle of Jameson's and worked on a funding letter.

It was foreign land to him. He had always invested his time into creating work as opposed to using his time seeking help funding his work. That normally manifested in getting a second job to cover the costs of a production. He had always operated with the agreement to actors that if he made money he would split it evenly. But it was community theatre in The City of NO, there was never any money gained. It was always a losing proposition, especially in the aftermath of The Catastrophe: they were artists spinning out of control with PTSDs trying to create and to reflect and to be beautiful in all of the ugliness. They gathered around scripts to disappear into imaginary skin to forget being homeless, isolated, thrown-away. They found joy in rehearsals because rehearsals were necessarily intimate and their lives had been obliterated.

The necessary bonds that come with a theatrical production were lifelines during those years. Henry, being a self-producing playwright, gave community when there was none. He, like them all, was heroic. Like most of those people, that time was gone, though. They were not remembered. The New Population artists erased all they had done. Now, Henry, perhaps being an adult, had bought a house and was trying to understand the concepts of Happy without being tethered to the city that had left him behind. Maybe at forty Henry was finally growing-up. He burned the first two versions of the letter.

After finishing the third version he put his good fist through the wall. He punched it intelligently, though. He struck it where he knew there were no studs. "It's not tragic," he told himself. "That entire side of the room needs redecoration."

The fourth version happened in the middle of the night when the bottle of whiskey was half empty. He wrote it on tissue paper with intentions of wiping his ass with it.

The fifth version he recited and fell in love with. However by the time he found a pen to write it down he had forgotten its most poignant lines.

He wrote the sixth and final version sitting on the side porch in the easy moments of first light. The very act of putting it into an envelope made him happy.

# 5

HENRY met with the owner/manager of the Marigny Theatre on St. Claude Avenue in The City of NO. He had had plays produced there before and liked the space. More importantly, though, it was a recognized theatre in the gay community which meant a built-in audience with, in the least, cursory free advertising. In the past he had always been able to get rehearsal space for free as part of the deal, too. 'Free' in the theatre world was a rare and lovely and illusive creature.

"You can't do it here. I'm booked," the owner told Henry. "There is a private club next door you can use for rehearsal if you're interested. I don't own it but I go there. I'll ask the guy and till then you can use the drag stage in the bar. Just do it in the mornings before the lunch crowd comes in. You'll have to pay for the space next door. It won't be much; charging you is more out of principle than anything. I'll show you then you can decide."

The place had an antechamber with a small counter for the business end of it, a few shelves of books for sale along with sexual aids: dildos, whips, cuffs, condoms, lube. The actual club was an S & M dungeon. There was a blend of scenarios and devices from clinical to traditional bondage. In the middle was a small sitting area. There was enough room to rehearse if the sitting area was rearranged.

"Can you do $150.00 a month? It's not a gay crowd that comes here, if that's what you were thinking. It's mostly straight professionals so you don't have to worry about an Eagle situation...."

Confounded, and feeling sorry for himself because sometimes writers lament the fact they can never live in the worlds they create and are stuck in the worlds they are forced to survive in, Henry drove Highway 90 back to the coast. He stopped for a few minutes before he got to the Rigolets because he felt like Jayne Mansfield might still visit from time to time the place where she was torn from the world.

He had a bottle of champagne in the car he had bought to share with her. He poured some on the ground, then took a drink; poured some on the ground, then took a drink. "Maybe being an artist is a foolish thing to be now," he said to Jayne. "Maybe that's what's to be learned, finally and once and for all, from The Catastrophe: our time is done in this town.

What do you think? Maybe we'll do something different now. Maybe we'll move forward with a new adventure and remember all this as something we did because we believed we had something to say that was needed. Hindsight is 20/20; maybe we've always been irrelevant. What do you think, Jayne? More champagne? More champagne."

He stopped for lunch at McDonalds in Waveland. The champagne filled his bladder.

He turned on the water in the sink, it sometimes made it easier to get a stream. He was standing at the urinal, water running, eyes closed trying to not think about any of the small catastrophes.

A nurse and an old black man came in. The old man was trying to make his way with a walker. The nurse followed at his side. The bathroom was too small to accommodate the entire operation so the nurse took the walker and left it outside in the dining area. He helped the old black man to the urinal next to Henry.

The old man tried to open his fly and muttered he couldn't. The arthritis in his hands was too bad.

"It's okay, Pop," the nurse said, "I've got you." Then the nurse stepped-up behind the old man, wrapped his arms around him, and opened his fly so the old man could piss.

The old man fell back against the nurse, leaned his head back onto his shoulder, looked up at the ceiling, "Praise God," he said.

"I've got you, Pop," the nurse said.

"Thank you, Jesus," the old man muttered with a trembling voice as he started a stream.

The nurse never wavered and wore him like a shadow.

Henry made it out of the bathroom and into the parking lot before he threw-up. Then he got mad at himself for being melodramatic. *Henry, you stupid son-of-a-bitch*, he told himself. *You just saw your future in The City of NO. There. Be grateful for clarity and stop being such a goddamned drama queen.*

Then he sat on the curb by the door and emptied the rest of his guts before he was able to laugh at how ridiculous he was being and make his way home.

When he got home he sat in the middle of the empty living room staring at the map of Indiana and The Fuck You Wall. He sipped whiskey from a new bottle of Jameson's. He drank and thought, drank and thought. And as he began to dance with the whiskey in his head he thought about the National Guardsman and Fear. *Over half of my life has been spent in Fear, in hiding,* he said to No One. Growing up gay in a time of Genocide, in a Southern Baptist family, living through his teens under the assumption of being less, it all came rushing back to him. The stress coursed underneath his skin, through the musculature, and into the marrow of the bone that had been put back together with pins. *I would have been a good preacher. I'm sorry, God.* He drank till it all went black.

When Henry Gereighty woke amongst the piss and vomit and empty whiskey bottle he saw clearly and in his flash of clarity he saw his new purpose before him along the blank wall of his empty living room. It was as if God had finally shined a light before him to guide him out of the muck and mire. Before making coffee, or shitting, or taking a shower in the outside stall that he loved he took the red marker and added an extensive list of people to The Fuck You Wall; everyone he could remember from a lifetime spent being the target of Hatred. When he had finished he turned to the empty facing wall, the one where God shone the light, and moved the ladder to reach the highest place.

Then, at the top of the empty facing wall he wrote: The Piss Map. The God-given vision was the clearest thing he had ever seen.

He stood back happily looking up to it.

Thaddeus' rocks bounced off the metal roof and shook Henry from the forming world of his new creation. He started coffee brewing, showered in the outside stall, then went back to the living room to inspect the genesis of his Future. With a clearer head he began to draw a map of the United States. He would draw, close his eyes to see the details in his mind's eye; draw, look back inside, then draw some more. It was not a lovely child's innocent ideation kind of map. It covered the entire wall: fourteen feet by twenty feet. In many ways it was magnificent: the size, the fact that he used all the colors he had – the coasts were all blue, and the mountain states were green; the Mojave was brown, and the rest were a tapestry made from all the colors of the rainbow. After he had finished the map he made his way to Walmart for a couple of cases of Mason Jars. The details of his vision were meticulous. It was as if the events had already happened and he was simply retracing them.

For the next three days he drank as much as his bladder could hold so that he would be able to piss in all the jars. After they were all filled and capped he created the hand written labels. When he finished his jaw hurt from grinding his teeth:

'To be poured onto the grave of

_____

in the event I die before I have
the opportunity to piss
on their headstone in person.'

The original list of people designated to get pissed on came from The Fuck You Wall and was pretty extensive:

Ronald Reagan, Jerry Falwell, Terry Dolan, Senator Kenneth Wherry, Senator Joseph McCarthy, Roy Cohn, J. Edgar Hoover, Whittaker Chambers, George W. Bush, Senator Larry Craig, Charlie Crist, Senator Jim McCrery, Congressman David Drier, Ed Koch, and Anita Bryant. Perhaps it should be the ultimate road trip for every gay man and woman in the country to travel from graveyard to graveyard, to piss on each one of them. In the wash of fag piss pink wildflowers would sprout to mock the memories of hatreds still encased in bone, anticipating their moment of resurrection.

Swimming in The Piss Map euphoria, he Googled the places where Ronald Reagan and Jerry Falwell were buried and marked them with gold sticker stars and the numbers 1 and 2 to create a sequence of gravestones to piss on. For the first time in his life, at the age of forty, Henry Gereighty felt truly, absolutely, positively, unmistakably, and passionately alive.

# 6

ON the day following the euphoric day on which Henry Gereighty gave birth to The Piss Map, Henry drove into The City of NO to meet with an actor. On the drive over he cajoled himself, convincing his mind what his heart already knew as fact.

*This drive is a waste of time, Henry.*

I love my new play.

*The play is not the thing.*

A year of my life...

*...that got you to this and this is better than that.*

That's still to be determined. So you're saying we just walk away from an entire year of work, hard work by the way?

*Look at it like research, the foundation for what's to come. Nothing's wasted here.*

I should have never become an artist; what a profound waste of time.

*This drive is the only waste of time. What you're doing now is the waste of time, not what you've done or what you're to become. What you've done has been perfect.*

Surely the non-artistic life is a happier life.

*Shut up, Henry.*

God I hate this drive.

<br>

"It's good to see you, Henry," the actor, Phillip, said. "I had written you off as having escaped this town. But here you are, you hard-headed son-of-a-bitch. You look like shit. Let me guess,..."

"Look I need a favor, Phil."

"Of course you do that's why you called me."

"I have this new play,..." Henry said.

"You have a new play. You always have a new play. You're a hard-headed son-of-a-bitch; God's own writer. The Little Playwright Who Could but Never Has. What a fucking riot. Please tell me it's a cabaret this time. This town has moved beyond your poetics; this is a lights-camera-action dick swinging town now, my friend; no more of the serious high-poetry shit that nobody comes to see. These New Population People like easily resolvable shiny packages. I hope you drove over here to tell me you've written a cabaret of swinging dick entitled *Naked Boys Singing, Part 2.* Please God. Let's make some money with this shit once and for all, Henry. We'll make bank then all of the plays over the years would have been for something. We'll convince ourselves they were all prep for our debut into the cabaret and we weren't wasting any time after all."

"Everything we've done has been good and for a reason."

"Calm down, Pricilla. I've been working with you all these years because I know you're good. You just haven't found your way. Your way is sex; that's what your way is. You're a talented gay writer for the love of God write about sex and make money. A talented gay writer who lives in poverty to write poetry? Really, Henry? Snap out of it already! Write naked, gay, writhing, nipple twisting, cock pulling sex, with a happy fruitalicious soundtrack and I'll be the happiest motherfucker on the planet."

"Actually it's a ghost play, something more mystical."

"Mystical. That's good, Henry. That's really great. A mystical ghost play. You write beautifully but you don't write well. Were you aware of that, Henry? As you're concocting all of these mystical ghost plays has it ever occurred to you that you're not getting anywhere? Use your God-given talent to write a hilarious musical that's filled with homo dick: big, swinging, shaved homo dick."

"I was thinking we'd start with a table read; get a couple of actors together, something casual, drinks, maybe some food, to read it and have a discussion. Then use that as the launching event towards a production."

"The usual," Phillip said.

"The usual," Henry said.

"Be sure and tell your landlord you won't be paying the rent anytime soon," Phillip said.

"Can I count on you to come onboard with this?" Henry said.

"Look, Henry, you've been gone again. You fucking disappear to write and expect to come back with a new play in your hand and have the world be as it was when you left it. The world moved on this time. If you're going to participate now you've got to reinvent yourself.

"I'm a writer: alone is a necessary liability."

"These new theatre companies pay, Henry."

"I'm trying to find money."

"These New Population Actors won't work for free, Henry. You've got me but I don't know what we'll be able to do about getting the others. This goddamned town is becoming cost-prohibitive. You haven't been around. A lot's happened in a year. There are fewer theatre spaces and the ones that are operable don't come cheap. The actors we used before are all movie extras now. Twenty-five dollars a day plus lunch trumps poetry and the poverty of artistic expression."

"I was only out of the loop for a year."

"A year's all it took."

"What about my new play, Phil?"

"If a playwright writes a new play and no one sees it did it ever exist to begin with? You missed the train, and now here you are."

"I love this play," Henry said.

"You no longer have clout. This is a film town now. If you can't pay your actors you have to at least produce a script they can use as an unofficial audition piece in the minute event somebody from the film industry comes to see it: predictable, marketable, shiny packages. No more of your experimental crap. No more amateur."

"Swinging dick," Henry said.

"Big, shaved, manscaped, homo dick, with a fruitalicious soundtrack."

# 7

AFTER leaving Phillip The Actor, Henry made his way towards Lower Decatur Street for a drink. He stopped on Chartres Street long enough to punch a brick wall. He normally carried a handkerchief and tape in his pocket. After punching the wall and getting rid of the frustrations he wrapped and taped up his bleeding knuckles and resumed the mission for a drink.

"You have nice eyes," Henry told the bartender who was ignoring him.

There was no response. He said it again, "You have nice eyes."

"What the hell is wrong with you?" The bartender said.

"You have nice eyes," Henry said again.

The bartender smiled a wry smile and looked Henry over. "Alright. You have a beautiful smile," he told Henry.

"You've got good arms," Henry said.

"Tell me about them," the bartender said.

"They're like sculpture; the good kind of sculpture, though."

"Italian?" The bartender said.

"Of course," Henry said.

"Your jeans make your ass look great," the bartender said.

"It's a great ass regardless of the clothes," Henry said.

"Do you want a drink?" The bartender said.

"Is it on you?" Henry said.

"I'll buy you a drink," the bartender said.

"A Compari and soda."

"Compari? Do you always drink things that taste like shit?" The bartender said.

"Yes," Henry said. "I'm sophisticated that way."

"Are you married?" The bartender said.

"No."

"Then I'm Frankie."

"Henry."

"Good to meet you, Henry."

"Same here, Frankie."

Frankie made the Compari and soda.

"Go out with me," Henry said.

"Why should I?"

"Because you have nice eyes and I have a beautiful smile and you have great arms and I have a nice ass. We complement one another."

"You're not an actor are you?" Frankie said. "I've lost my tolerance for actors and film people."

"I'm not an actor."

"I'm a normal guy," Frankie said.

"I'm a normal guy," Henry said back.

"I'd like to see you tonight," Frankie said.

"I'd like to see you tonight and in the morning," Henry said.

"You're looking for an all-nighter?" Frankie said.

"Depends on the chemistry," Henry said.

"I want to see you tonight and in the morning and possibly at lunch if we both still think it's a good idea and the chemistry holds out," Frankie said.

"Leave work now," Henry said.

"Where do you live?" Frankie said.

"Deal breaker: Mississippi coast, Pass Christian."

"I'm in the Treme."

"I love the Treme."

"There are too many white people now, the gumbo's been watered down by all these film people. Selah."

"Don't change the subject on me."

"It wasn't my intention. I struggle with wrapping my head around all the changes," Frankie said.

"I like pancakes and that's all I care about at the moment," Henry said.

"I've got a mix."

"I like to put molasses in the batter," Henry said.

"I've got a new box of Aunt Jemima just-add-water batter, and a shiny new jar of Brer Rabbit molasses and I love to spoon," Frankie said.

"I want to fuck and have pancakes in bed and spoon and sleep in till we wake up without an alarm," Henry said. "And I no longer care about what's happening in The City of NO."

"And then what do you want?" Frankie said. "After sleeping in?"

"Depends on the chemistry."

# 8

HENRY kissed Frankie as passionately as he had ever kissed anyone because he had been filled with worth and sometime ago he forgot that was something he innately possessed. Freshly fucked, he made his way back to the coast.

Henry, forever engaging in the world around him, regardless of his better judgment, pulled off the I-10 in Slidell to piss.

There were two urinals and a stall. Some guy was taking a shit while his buddy was pissing. Henry gave him a bro-nod, flushed the pisser and unzipped, concentrating to get a fast stream. He had a hard time pissing in public restrooms.

"You know, it's like I was saying," the pissing redneck said. "I'm not a Bible thumper or anything, but I just don't think being a faggot is what God wants for anybody."

Henry sighed, and said: "That's what you were talking about? Right before I walked in, you were standing there with your dick in your hand, chatting up your buddy, talking about God and fags?"

"Yes, sir, and that's when you walked in. I'm a fag magnet."

"Oh fuck off," Henry The Pain Junkie said.

The guy in the stall started to laugh.

The pissing redneck didn't respond. He had no experience with victims fighting back.

Henry relaxed and started a stream and said, "Stupid fucking redneck."

The guy in the shitter burst out laughing so the pissing redneck backhanded Henry. It was a good solid blow and sent Henry against the wall. He caught himself before he fell, pissing on his pants leg.

Henry's ear was ringing as Redneck quickly pulled him up and slammed him against the wall.

He closed his eyes to concentrate on the endorphin rush.

The guy came out of the stall and washed his hands. "Okay, you've proved your point," he said to Redneck as he left. "Let's go get something to eat."

Redneck let him go and was leaving when Henry said, "You don't wash your hands after you piss, pig?"

Redneck stopped, turned, took the few steps back to Henry, and slugged him in the face.

Henry closed his eyes again to feel it.

"You must feel right at home in here," the redneck said, "bleeding and humiliated in a truck stop bathroom..."

His buddy opened the door, "I said let's go, I'm hungry."

Redneck washed his hands, dried them off on Henry's shirt tail, then left.

Henry sat in his car and cleaned off his face.

*One of these times some son-of-a-bitch is going to kill you.*

You think I don't know that?

*You could be more careful.*

How do you propose I do that? Wear a rubber suit?

*This whole 'Ballad of the Self-Loathing Homosexual' thing you've got going on is getting pretty old.*

I just concentrate on the endorphins. It's not as tragic as you make it out.

*Yes, you're a real bruiser.*

I prefer warrior.

He dialed Frankie. The pumping adrenaline made it difficult to punch the phone numbers: "Call in sick to the bar and come to the coast and spend the night with me. I want to kiss you again."

Back at his house, as he waited for Frankie, Henry busied himself inventorying the jars of piss. In doing the inventory he felt better about life in general.

Frankie, with a case of wine in his hands, knocked on the door with his foot. "You sounded a little rattled on the phone," he said as he surveyed the damage to Henry's face. "What's the matter? Are you and Mississippi about to break-up?"

"This was Louisiana," Henry said.

"Those two bitches are always trying to outdo one another."

"Come in and make yourself comfortable," Henry said.

"Nice house," Frankie said as he stood before the Piss Map. "Graffiti artist?"

"Sometimes therapy, sometimes an aspiration."

# 9

THEY split a bottle of the cheap French red while Henry fried fish and potatoes to take with them in the little boat.

"The Fuck You Wall I get. The Piss Map, I don't know about that one."

"It's practical application. The Fuck You Wall is ever changing. The Piss Map is forever."

"What kind of therapist hooked you up with those two coping mechanisms? I'm asking out of envy. I'd like their number."

"The product of violence and whiskey."

"You're a little twisted, aren't you?"

"I prefer to think of it as an accurate response to decades of bad things," Henry said. He scooped some fish from the skillet, blew on it, and tasted it, then said, "Open up, mon vieux," as he fed Frankie a bite. "What do you think?"

"Needs Crystals," Frankie said.

"Exactly what I was about to say."

"Are you going to go to those places you've got marked on the map?"

"Right now it makes me feel good and that's all I care about. It feels good to fight back, in whatever capacity, right?"

"Here's to you," Frankie said in a toast.

The Gulf of Mexico was normally flat along the Pass Christian coastline and some days dolphins would leap from the water and race and have water fights. It was that kind of day. The two men filled the little boat with the case of wine, fishing gear, and food then carried it into the water. They walked out twenty yards or more till the water was thigh deep then they climbed in and paddled out. Except for an easy breeze it was overcast and still. Somewhere close and inland there was a pocket of rain and they could smell freshness in the air. The paddling was easy as they watched the dolphins.

Everything about catching tuna for them was luck of the draw: it wasn't bigger than they both could handle, there was a gaff onboard; and Henry, unsure of a stranger on the boat, had a substantial knife.

In filleting the fish they were careful to not drop anything overboard. The bullhead sharks along the northern coast of the Gulf are aggressive. In another stroke of luck Henry had trash bags onboard for the guts. Eating fish straight from the water was euphoric. The meat tasted like blood and salt and life and both the men ate well.

"They pay big money for this all over the world and by-god here we get it for free and free makes it even better," Frankie said.

"It's good," Henry said.

"Free makes it better."

"Cut me another chunk."

"I feel very French right now," Frankie said.

"You're last name's St. Pierre. You were smart to bring the whole case of red, Mister St. Pierre."

Frankie tried to stand to piss over the side.

"Do you have to stand up to do that? Can't you get up on your knees and pull it off? You're going to tip us over."

"Goddamn you complain a lot," Frankie said.

"We're officially 'at sea.' I don't feel like swimming back."

"Nobody's going to be swimming anywhere. We're not going to tip over, even if I stand up and piss. She's a good boat, nice and beamy. We haven't gone to sea in a pirogue, Mister Gereighty."

Henry pontificated as Frankie pissed: "Look at it, Frankie; you can barely see anything of the land. We're no longer a part of anything but us."

"And it's a good day."

"I claim you," Henry said.

"That's very good of you. What is it that you're going for here?"

"In this moment you are my country, my state and city; my address. I claim you and nothing or nobody else."

"That's fucking silly."

"The good kind of silly."

"Here," Frankie said leaning over with a chunk of the raw fish in his fingers.

Henry opened his mouth.

Frankie fed him, then said, "I guess today, in this moment, we get to be fucking silly."

The men were jarred awake by seagulls diving the little boat for a chunk of the fish meat on the carcass of the half-eaten tuna. The boat and the men were covered in dried salt and blood. Low-tide had left them beached in four inches of water and mud. Somehow during the course of the trip, one of them had scrawled onto the side of the dingy SS La Vielle Ferme, then on the stern the name Rose.

"I have to piss again," Frankie said as he stood up to piss over the side.

"I think it's okay if you get out of the boat to do that now."

Frankie stepped out of the boat, into the muddy water, and pissed. Then stepped back into the boat and sat down. "I think I just walked on water," he said.

Even though they were beached they had not yet returned to the world because they were enveloped in a bank of fog.

"I would bathe in champagne if I could afford it," Henry said.

"We can call this champagne," Frankie said.

"That'd be no good. It's cheap red. We'll call it cheap red and bathe in it. Hold your mouth open, Frankie."

Frankie leaned his head back and Henry poured the wine into his throat. Then he splashed some over his hand and rubbed it over his face, chest, and arms, cleaning off the sweat and dried salt. "I will bathe you in red wine till we can afford champagne," Henry said.

"It's a bitch being a poor elitist," Frankie said.

A cacophony of seagulls surrounded the happy drunk men.

The next morning the gimp rained rocks onto the roof of Henry's house.

Frankie jumped out of bed first. "They're shooting at us!"

"Nobody's shooting at us," Henry said to Frankie then clamored out of bed, made his way through the shotgun house then out the front door. "Goddammit, Thaddeus!" He said as he stepped outside and a rock caught him in the mouth.

"I know what you are!" Thaddeus yelled then ran down the tracks, bellowing with laughter.

"Nobody's shooting at us," Henry said to Frankie.

"Let me guess, the local representative of the Mississippi

Welcome Wagon," Frankie said.

"Mississippi and Homo's are natural born enemies. Interestingly enough the most redneck homophobic Mississippi native would drop to his knees in a heartbeat for the opportunity to blow Brett Favre. I think it's that inner conflict that keeps them so disagreeable."

Frankie slinked up to the tracks and filled his backpack with rocks. He put them on the side porch and then he and Henry had coffee and waited. It wasn't long before the first few rocks landed on the metal roof. The sound set Frankie and Henry into motion. The men headed around the house and waited till Thaddeus was directly in front of them on the tracks.

Thaddeus was pummeling the little house. Then the boys let loose. The sounds that came from Thaddeus were hideous: the squeal of a small girl mixed with the cries of a wounded cat. He gathered the cape over his head for a canopy and flailed his arms as he ran from the tracks, around the cemetery, and behind the sweet olive trees to the safety of his own yard.

The boys sat in the grass and laughed. It was good laughter, the kind that made them hold their bellies. Then, after they could stand, they went back inside, to the kitchen, and cooked breakfast. They sat on the front porch, in the first moments of direct sunlight, and ate the plantains and tilapia. As they finished breakfast they could hear a train heading their way. And as quickly as the first sounds of the rumbling it was passing; shining silver cars, one after the other, with Barnum and Baileys Circus painted on the metal. And from time to time, there would be someone standing outside a car smiling and waving at them. It was beautiful and both of the men felt an excitement stirring inside of themselves that perhaps they hadn't felt in twenty years and it reminded them of innocence and they were happy.

After Frankie had gone Henry stood the ladder up against the fourth wall in the living room and, with a blue marker in his hand, climbed to the top. He wrote, Those In Good Standing; then underneath that he wrote: 1. Parents; 2. Brother; 3. Frankie St. Pierre.

# 10

THERE were gunshots close enough to hear casings hit the concrete. A summer storm was moving in as Henry stepped inside the cowboy bar. Everything smelled like rain and the constant breeze moving the front inland towards the pine belt made the humidity bearable. Frankie was behind the bar.

"Did you hear the shots?" Henry said to Frankie.

"Another drug dealer shot another drug dealer and the NOPD are nowhere to be found. You didn't tell me you were coming by tonight."

"I didn't realize I had to," Henry said. "I thought I'd swing by and take you to dinner. Do you want to go to dinner?"

"Am I supposed to feel obligated to?" Frankie said.

"You shouldn't ever feel obligated to do anything. I don't."

"If you drove over here that's on you," Frankie said.

"Is there something happening that I should know about?" Henry said.

"I'm not your boyfriend, Henry," Frankie said.

"I never said you were. I drove over to spend some time with you because I wanted to do that. It has nothing to do with you. It's about what I want. If you're not into it say so."

"I'll have dinner with you. I want everything to be clear. That's all."

"It's clear," Henry said.

Then Frankie said, "Let's go to the Quarter and take a walk and eat where we feel like it. How does that sound?"

"I'm starting to lose my appetite," Henry said.

"I'll buy you a drink while I finish things up here. By then you'll have it back."

The men climbed into Henry's car and drove the couple of blocks to Chartres Street in the Marigny and parked. Somehow to both of them it felt safer now having mobilized from ground zero of the shooting. They crossed Esplanade and headed into the Quarter. As they made their way across the neutral ground it started to rain.

"I like it when it's like this," Henry said.

Frankie opened his umbrella.

"I want to walk in the rain," Henry said.

"Suit yourself. The umbrella will be for me."

"Did something happen to piss you off? I thought we had a great time the last time I saw you."

"We did have a great time," Frankie said. "Probably one

of the best times I've ever had. I don't want to be your boyfriend."

"You're not. We already said that," Henry said.

"I don't want you to get too comfortable and I don't want that for me either," Frankie said.

"You're here for me to kiss on: instant boyfriend, flavor of the month, friend with benefits; whatever you want to call it," Henry said. "No commitment. I thought that's what we were doing."

"It is and that's all it is," Frankie said.

"Then we're on the same page," Henry said.

"We're on the same page," Frankie said. "I didn't ask for you to drive over here to see me."

"I did it because I wanted to see you. Anything else? Are the boundaries clear enough now?"

"You can use the umbrella if you change your mind," Frankie said.

"I told you I like walking in the rain."

Chartres Street was nearly empty except for them. The few tourists who were out stood in doorways and huddled under eaves to keep some part of them dry. Henry and Frankie walked in the street, Frankie under the umbrella and Henry with his head leaning back so the rain washed over his face. As they walked Henry took Frankie's hand in his. Frankie pulled back and slapped his hand away.

"No PDAs," Frankie said.

They walked a few minutes more till Henry took Frankie's hand in his. Again, Frankie pulled back and slapped his hand away.

"No PDAs," Frankie said.

That's how they walked through the quarter until they felt hungry and turned into a place for a beer and bowl of gumbo.

"I like that you're a little scrappy," Frankie said. "It's a turn on: real man."

"As opposed to a fake one?"

"I like brawn and musk and a guy who isn't afraid to fight if he has to," Frankie said.

"I thought you liked me because I made the first move," Henry said.

"Making an effort racked up a lot of points right off the bat," Frankie said.

"Do you play the guitar?" Henry said.

"I don't play any instruments," Frankie said.

"If you could play the guitar it would be easier to like you for real as opposed to liking you enough to fuck."

"You like me for real," Frankie said. "I can tell."

"And so what if I do? I'd never say it out loud; it'd scare you off," Henry said.

"Are we going to pretend we're investing to make this more fun?" Frankie said.

"I'm going to move forward like we're moving and not think about anything like that. I'm going to enjoy you and not think about anything more than the Right Now. I hope you're going to do the same."

"How do you feel about polyamory?" Frankie said.

"Is that some kind of plastic toy, like a Fleshlight?" Henry said.

"Real funny; maybe what I'd like from you is to like you and be able to count on you and have that same thing with somebody else; or maybe a couple of somebody elses," Frankie said. "I think that may be what I'm looking for."

"You don't know what you're looking for in me, Frankie?"

"I'm thinking about the bigger picture," Frankie said. "The older I get the more it seems that is the only reasonable response in the Year of our Lord, 2008; better than being alone. I feel like I'm convincing myself. This is getting deep. I don't want to get into deep conversation. I've noticed you like to do that. That's not what I'm good for. I don't like hanging out with you to have deep conversations. Change the subject. The checkout girls at the Winn Dixie say I look like Harry Connick, Jr. Now you tell me something about you. Tell me about your first relationship."

"You don't look like Harry Connick, Jr."

"I never said I did. I said the checkout girls at the Winn Dixie said I did."

"I came out in my early 30s. I was in a play. ..."

"If Harry Connick, Jr. had been raised in poverty then

he and I would look similar," Frankie said. "I look like the impoverished version of Harry Connick, Jr. What? Don't look at me like that. Everybody knows the poor and the wealthy age differently. They exist in different countries."

"Are you finished telling your story now?" Henry said.

"Are you being curt with me?" Frankie said.

"Like I was saying: my first boyfriend, he was a film guy slumming, running the lighting board for this play I had a part in. It lasted off and on for about three years."

"That's it?"

"We've been friends for more than a decade now," Henry said.

"You're not a long-term relationship kind of a guy, are you? See, right there, proof of a polyamorous bent," Frankie said. "My first and only relationship with a man lasted seven years; before that I was married for twenty. He was a younger college professor, had a wife and kids. It's a terrible situation to try and love someone in. That wasn't here, though. I met him in San Francisco. I left the south as soon as I divorced. I wanted to be somewhere where I wouldn't feel like a freak while I was learning what it means to be gay. The relationship I had with him would never happen in this town, ever. Every gay man should leave the south as quickly as possible. The south destroys gay men. Go, learn about who you are and when you're strong, however long it takes, then come back home if you'd like. Come back and change things and make them better for everyone that comes after you." All that said, Frankie noticed how Henry was looking at him, there was a hint of admiration in the stare. "Why are you looking at me like that?"

"I'm always impressed with passion," Henry said. "I just didn't expect it from you."

"It's better to not expect anything from anybody, and the conversation's getting too deep again," Frankie said.

"Do we know enough about each other now to feel comfortable that neither one of us will take The Gay Way out of this affair?" Henry said.

"Are all writers so analytical?" Frankie said.

"I've never been called that before," Henry said.

"What? A writer?"

"Analytical. Usually I get called Dreamer but in the bad way," Henry said. "I won't disappear on you without any word, or trace. When I'm done with this whatever-we're-doing, I'll say goodbye."

"I appreciate that, Henry," Frankie said. "If we weren't in a restaurant right now I'd lean over the gumbo and kiss you."

# 11

Mr. Henry Gereighty
213 E. Railroad St.
Pass Christian, MS
Re: Artist Sponsorship Request

Mr. Gereighty;

We were excited to receive and read your proposal for 501c3 support for your latest theatre endeavor. We are aware of your work and commitment to re-building the Arts in the city and applaud your efforts, as well as value your continuing contributions with your newest play "Chapeau Tombe Nan La Mer."

It is an exciting time in the city of New Orleans and along the Gulf Coast and we've taken on the leadership position of spearheading this cultural renaissance. We're reinventing the theatre and have the utmost confidence the next ten years are going to establish the Crescent City as a national theatre hub. We are reaching out to inform you of our plans and hope you will offer us your support. We at PAC have decided to go a different, bolder route this season, taking into consideration what we see as being the best for future growth in the performing arts in this city.

We've taken on supporting a new and exciting theatrical company based in Chicago with hopes we'll be able to build a bridge between them and us over the next year. We've been hard at work creating a feeder artist program in the Windy City to establish a pipeline for artists to support our transformation. Obviously it's an enormous and ambitious undertaking. We welcome your support and know that in the coming years local playwrights like yourself will have much to learn and gain from this collaboration.

Best of luck to you, Mr. Gereighty. And please do keep us informed on the progress of your work.

Yours Truly,

—————————————
Performing Arts Consortium, Gulf Coast Division
811 Camp Street
New Orleans, LA

Henry read the letter several times before driving to The City of NO to see Frankie. He called him from the road; no answer. He left a message. "It's me, Frankie; I'm headed over. I'd like to see you tonight. I need to see you tonight. Are you around? Call me back and say you're around. I really need to talk to someone and I'd like that someone to be you."

Frankie didn't return the call. He sent the same text. There was no response. He stopped off at the bar. Frankie called in sick for his shift. He went by his apartment in the Treme. Frankie wasn't there.

# 12

EVERYONE should have a relationship with their country. There should be a bond of trust, of community, an ineffable knowledge of belonging. But those things only work in written declarations. In the southern gay world, the Children of Genocide remained harbingers of distrust and self-destruction. People like Henry, who had always moved through their lives with that knowing, stayed true to the innate need for community, as ideal as it was, and as constructed inside the walls of their forts. They lived alone. The Catastrophe decimated any semblance of community they had spent their lives building. Their lives happened on fiery landscapes. Their borders were forever under attack and being redefined: some days more land, some days less land; battle by battle, from trench to trench along the ramparts that protected the walls constructed more than thirty years earlier. Some of them, like Henry, could see the flames and smell the smoke; they lived on the battlefields striving to become adept at dodging bullets; the others, most of the population, retreated long ago and their eyes had adjusted to living in the darkness, morphed into blind fish in stagnant ponds. The loss of community was perhaps the greatest loss from The Catastrophe. Since Henry's retreat to the coast in the wake of a hate crime he had been boiling to simply talk. On this night in the middle of summer, with Frankie nowhere to be found, Henry walked into Pravda on Lower Decatur Street. The beautiful little bar in crimson drapes was virtually vacant.

"I need to be heard and I need to feel good," Henry said. "Would you listen to me complain?"

The guy wearing a bowtie and suspenders was the only person in the bar. "For $20.00 I'll listen to you complain."

"My Instant Boyfriend is nowhere to be found and I feel too alone to go home," Henry said.

"If this is the complaining part of your plan I haven't yet agreed to hear it."

"It's not."

"I'll give you my undivided attention for 30 minutes for $20.00. It's a discounted rate because of the heat and all. You'll give the bartender a $20.00 bill up front to hold as my fee, plus an additional $5.00 for his trouble. That's the way it'll work. Take it or leave it."

"Do I get a drink out of the deal?" Henry said.

"Only if you buy your own. It's a Dutch affair."

Henry looked around the bar. There were just a couple of people in the place; it was mid-week and summer. The young, twink bartender was busy on Facebook. "Thirty full minutes," he said.

"It's a business deal. I'll write it out, we'll both sign it. You can set the timer on your phone. You should, actually; to make sure neither one of us are cheated."

Henry gave the bartender twenty-five dollars and set his timer for 30 minutes.

"Don't start the timer just yet, let me piss first. I can't very well give you my undivided attention if my eyes are floating, now can I? When I get back we'll put it in writing."

The guy pissed, came back and wrote the details of the event on a napkin. Both men signed it. They both ordered drinks so the half hour session wouldn't be interrupted by drink orders.

With new drink in hand, the guy said, "Commence to complain."

And Henry did. As he began to talk, a floodgate opened. It was the first time since The Catastrophe he had had the opportunity to speak without conversation being a competitive sport. Lower Decatur Street lay out quiet in the throes of the late night summer swelter. The bored bartender yawned more than once in the background as Henry Gereighty remembered what it meant to actually talk about himself and have anyone listen. He spoke without the bullshit of agenda. He had 30 full minutes to expose who he was and be heard.

He began by bitching about the theatre in The City of NO; how that and everything else had changed so drastically in such a short period of time; how the City of New Orleans sank and The City of NO rose simultaneously; how he and all those like him had been erased by the new population of artists who had flocked to the place to create their own renaissance in the rubble. But that only took a minute. There was nothing to proselytize over. It was all factual, and being A Child of Genocide invisibility was within his comfort zone. He stated the facts and it was done. Surprisingly the other 29 minutes were filled with Ronald Reagan and Jerry Falwell, with the NIH and the CDC. "The President of the United States hated me," he said.

"The heads of State, newspapers, my teachers, my doctor, they hated me. Congress, Christian America, my mom and dad; they all hated me. So I stopped being me. They loved me when I stopped being me. I was just a kid." He ranted, and paced the bar, then flung his hands in the air, and shouted and screamed a primal scream till he lost his breath and sat down, gasping for air. "Fear has governed my entire life, all of it; waiting for my parents to die so that I could fill my lungs with free oxygen. How did I become such a god-damned coward?" Twenty-something years of unspoken hurt surged through his entire body, circling the bone that had been snapped in half, ricocheting around the inside perimeters of his skull, and flying out of his mouth with all the vitriol of every man, every southern man, who had ever lived a half-life, held captive inside their own hearts by hatreds. And who, now, watched their history being erased, utterly forgotten, by an enlightened generation.

When he had finished, he wiped the tears from his eyes, the spit from his mouth, and took his seat next to the guy who had listened to him. He raised his glass to the guy. "Thanks, man. I needed that."

"Indeed you did," the guy said.

They drank.

Then the guy said, "You and I could be friends."

"How much would that cost me?" Henry said.

He ordered two shots of Jameson and two pints of Guinness. "To being friends. It's okay. I'm a lawyer and I'm straight."

They shook hands.

"I like dick, and apparently I'm an ex-playwright," Henry said.

"Should we discuss religious affiliation next?" The lawyer said.

"Maybe we shouldn't push our luck," Henry said.

"That's funny; you're funny," the lawyer said. "Educate me."

"What's that?"

"Tell me about being an artist. I know nothing about it. I like knowledge."

"Then you must live a lonely life."

"You should be a stand-up," the lawyer said. "What's the difference between being a gay artist and a straight artist? There have to be differences, don't they?"

Henry choked on his beer. "Don't make me spit beer, man. Since The Storm the whole concept of friendship doesn't exist anymore, so we're not going to be friends. How's that? We're going to be drinking buddies. It's hard to disappoint a drinking buddy. I need a drinking buddy in my life. With that question you officially meet all the criteria of a drinking buddy, but the good kind of drinking buddy."

"There's a good and bad kind?"

"The good kind is non-superficial, is sincere; makes an effort."

"Exactly: Friends."

"No; listen to me slowly: one late, hot, and sad night..."

"Are you going to tell me a story?" The lawyer said.

"If you'd shut up and listen I am: one late, hot, and sad night in The Aftermath of The Catastrophe; as The City of NO was rising from the waters in all of its shining glory there were two jazz funerals. They were perhaps the largest jazz funerals in the history of such things. They both started in Jackson Square on the front steps of the St. Louis Cathedral. One headed down river, the other up river. They serpentined through the entire city and played as beautifully as anyone had ever played. The interesting part is that no one saw them, very few could even hear them. It takes a certain kind of person to see what's typically invisible, just because something is invisible does not mean it does not exist. The ones who could see and hear have never stopped weeping because they experienced the essence of what love actually can be. They were souls, the spirits of everyone past who has ever loved the City of New Orleans. There were too many to count. As the processions of the dead made their way through the streets there was barely enough room to move there were so many people. One coffin held Community, the other Redemption. Both were buried in the notes and concrete of St. Louis #1. 'Community' is dead. 'Friend' is dead. Don't be my friend; 'Friend' is dead."

"I'm going to change the subject."

"As any good drinking buddy would."

"The whole arts thing interests me," the lawyer said. "Personally I think it's come to be an irrelevant past-time; which makes it even more interesting. Is it correct to assume a gay artist and a straight artist are different animals, even as the whole thing has passed into the realm of cultural curiosity?"

"First off, fuck you...."

"You're welcome. I do love to incite passion," the lawyer said.

"Secondly, the differences are in the details of the work. A bad gay artist is the same as a bad straight artist: neither one understands their perspective, they have no voice. A good artist masters his voice to say all the things that are inside him in such a way that people are affected; and maybe some even changed. Gay artists and straight artists live in different countries. The truly great artists are the ones who are true to their own people and those of different lands simultaneously. The great ones transcend all the compartmentalization. There are very few of those."

"Are you one of those?" The lawyer said.

"Oh no; no, no, no. I'm way too damaged to be one of those guys," Henry said. "I'm a..." He stopped himself, then, "I 'was' a self-producing playwright. I wrote. I workshopped. I would cast. I directed. I built sets. I sold tickets. I designed advertisements. I hung lights and cut gels. I would tend bar in the lobby at intermission. I paid for everything and always lost money when it was all done. I endured actors."

"Why on earth would anyone do all of that?"

"Profound misunderstanding of Reasonable Sacrifice."

"Now it's all in the past."

"I've been A Recovering Playwright for less than 24 hours."

"Is there congratulation due?" The lawyer said.

"I think so. It feels right. Let's talk about you. I'm still tender."

"I sue people. The end," the lawyer said. "Artists fascinate me. They always have. What do you write about?"

"Past-tense, cowboy. I'm officially untethered to The Arts. The denizens of the New New Orleans have taken control at the helm; let Them and their ship called The City of NO have at it."

"You're not going down without a fight are you?" The lawyer said.

"I have a plan. They will get theirs, and I will get my revenge."

"You're not just going to walk away and leave it up to the myth of karma are you?" The lawyer said. "I hope you would at least take a swing and get your punches in while you can."

"The City of NO is driven by Chaos," Henry said. "Now, four years after The Catastrophe, Chaos is resting. But even while resting in the Captains Chambers, he listens; and from time to time he rears his ugly head in moments of spontaneous combustion throughout the belly, and along the decks, of the ship known as The City of NO. Those are reminders he still watches and waits till he's ready. When he's ready he'll strike; as he always has. The City of NO is visceral because Chaos is visceral. As the New Population becomes settled and confident they are the ones driving the ship, Chaos will rise from his slumber and come up from his chambers and seep into their brains and watch as they fumble over the decks and cross the halyards and set themselves up for their imminent demise. And, being of an orchestral bent, Chaos will play his violin to the rhythms of wood and bone crackling on his pyre, as he watches their lives burn down on his decks as they engulf in his flame; as he reclaims what's rightfully his; as the New Ones become the Old Ones with tired eyes and worn bodies lost in the passionate demise of the Pain Junkie. Goddamn The City of NO."

"So your plan is to beat them about the head and shoulders with your pages of poetry?"

"In the event I haven't yet told you to fuck off I'll do it now: fuck off."

"Now, see; that is exactly what I was talking about, although relegated to cultural curiosity, artists have relevance. Your relevance apparently is the poetic. That's like double-indemnity, isn't it? Aren't poets on the lowest rung of the economically viable? They're even lower than playwrights, aren't they? Why on earth would a gay man agree to the impoverished life of a poet? Don't you people have it bad enough the way it is? I hope for your sake somewhere in your catalog of writing you've been secretly working on *Naked Boys Singing, Part 2*. And I hope, too, after now becoming exacerbated by the cost-prohibitive nature of full productions of your poetry, you'll move forward with an economically viable venture. Isn't writing plays about being gay antiquated?"

"That was a huge assumption," Henry said. "Sexuality informs …'informed' my work. My work was never about sexuality. I wrote about people who are gay. It was a process designed to normalize."

"Please, it is 2008."

"And it is Louisiana. If there were any semblance of cohesion in the gay community, and I mean on a national level, Louisiana would be boycotted. Imagine it: homosexuals stop coming to New Orleans, period. Homosexuals stop spending money in this town. Imagine the economic impact that would have. Then, and only then, would there be strides towards true equality in this state."

"So you write about your experiences in the south?" The lawyer said seeming to be very proud of his powers of observation.

"Are all lawyers this assumptive?"

"'Assumptive,' good word," the lawyer said.

"That was condescending."

"Condescension is a tool of the trade for me. Tell me more about your experiences with the arts."

"Why should I?"

"I'm considering entertainment law. I like being entertained. You're a storyteller, whether you're still writing plays or not, aren't you? I imagine it's a lifelong vocation; something you do because it's what's inside of you. You stop telling them on the stage then you start telling them in a different medium. Is that right?"

"So far so good."

"So educate me," the lawyer said.

"All stories begin with the writer. Then the characters move into their own and leave him. They become something that he is not. After the separation they are equals and the story becomes a dialogue the writer documents. At least that's the way it is with successful stories. The pain in the necessary separation is why writers are addicts."

"So you're a gay, ex-playwright alcoholic?" The lawyer said. "That's not very original, is it?"

"Perhaps a high-functioning alcoholic," Henry said. "The jury is still out."

"Oh, nice," the lawyer said. "You made a courtroom reference for my benefit."

"Asshole," Henry said.

"Drinking buddy," the lawyer said.

Then they both raised their glasses and in tandem, as if rehearsed, said, "Not friends."

"How long have you been a lawyer?" Henry said.

"Ten years. I took the bar when I was thirty."

"Tell me this then: What are the legalities attached to pissing on tombstones?" Henry said.

"Now see, why can't people just be normal?" The lawyer said. "Is that too much to ask?"

"We're both perfectly normal, nice people," Henry said.

"Through the lens of a kaleidoscope we're normal," the lawyer said. "I wouldn't recommend desecrating a grave-yard. People get pissy about that kind of thing. You wouldn't want the legal system to make an example of you, as they are want to do."

"I'll do it at night. The whole thing will be clandestine."

"Whose grave are you going to be pissing on anyway?"

"I was thinking Reagan's."

"Oh, well, in that case just be careful."

"That was a fast turn-around."

"I'm malleable and desperately want to be liked. Tell me something else about you. What's your favorite word?"

"Motherfuck."

"That's brutal," the lawyer said.

"It's my favorite word," Henry said.

"You're not optimistic, are you?"

"And that's not like me. It's all different now. Maybe being a pessimist is my new norm. Tell me your favorite word," Henry said.

"Unicorn."

"And I'm the faggot," Henry said.

"You bring out my girl side," the lawyer said. "You make me feel young and pretty."

"Once again: Fuck off," Henry said. "And your word

doesn't count. Unicorn is a thing, not an informative word. Your favorite word can't be a noun."

"Technicality, and I never agreed to those rules. You can't make up rules as you go."

"Says the malleable one."

"It's occupational for me."

"Goddamn lawyer."

"Goddamn playwright."

"Ex-playwright, and Motherfuck." Then Henry stopped himself. He was becoming too familiar. *You're being as giddy as a schoolgirl, Henry.* He chided himself. *What the fuck? Are you this desperate for contact? 'I like you, do you like me, yes, no, or maybe?'* After beating himself he smiled, took a long drink, and said, "Saints fan?"

"Of course," the lawyer said. "That's a stupid fucking question." He took a long drink, too. Then he said, "Unicorn," and smiled. "Your favorite word is motherfuck?"

"Really, seriously, truly."

"It almost makes me sad for you."

"'Almost' being the operative word," Henry said getting up.

"Where are you going?"

"Bathroom, I'm prairie doggin'," Henry said. "Do you have somewhere to be tonight?"

"Nowhere but here," the lawyer said. "You?"

"I live on the coast. I'm going to spend the night here, bullshitting with you, then head over to Fiorella's for breakfast around daybreak. Then maybe take a swim in the Gulf around noon tomorrow. Sound like a plan?"

"Sounds like a plan," the lawyer said.

Henry came back from the crapper. He played Janice on the jukebox and pulled the lawyer off his stool. He took the lawyers hand in his and danced around him. Then he said, "Come on, Twink," to the bartender. The bartender took Henry's hand and the three men shook their asses as Janis wailed, and filled the beautiful little bar before her pounding voice rolled out the door onto the sticky heat wet late night sidewalks.

It was the dancing that lured the beautiful straight couple in.

"There's a party in here," the woman said. "A southern gentleman, a derelict, and a homosexual; and they all get along. It looks like goddamned New Orleans to me. Is there room for a new bride and her husband, the boxer?"

"I'm assuming," the lawyer said, "that I am the southern gentleman you're referring to."

"You're the only bowtie I see in this dive," she said.

"There's plenty of room, and congratulations," the lawyer said.

"It was three years ago," the boxer said.

"It's our three year anniversary," she said.

"Last week was three years," the boxer said.

"It's our three year anniversary month," she said. "A marriage is worth an annual month's celebration, isn't it?"

"Drinks for our new friends," the lawyer told the bartender who had climbed back behind the bar. "Four shots of the good rum."

"Whiskey," the woman said.

"Two shots of each," the lawyer told the bartender.

Henry shook hands with the boxer, "Henry Gereighty."

"You're not going to shake my hand?" The woman said.

The lawyer shook her hand.

"It wasn't really what I was going for," the woman said.

Then the shots were on the bar.

The lawyer raised his shot into the air, "Lady and Gentlemen, to new friends."

"We're friends already?" The woman said.

"We're friendly people like that," Henry said. Then he turned to the fighter, "To us."

"To us all," the lawyer said.

They all raised their glasses: "To new friends," and drank.

"I have a fascination with violence," Henry said to the fighter.

"I've never seen boxing as violence," the fighter said. "If it was just violence I couldn't have ever committed to it."

"Of course it's violent," the woman said. Then she told the lawyer, "I'm working on him. The man has a master's degree in political science but he prefers to beat people up."

"I lose as many as I win; it's primal artistry."

Henry ordered a round of drinks, "We've got to drink to that. Guinness okay for everybody?"

"Miller Lite," the woman said.

"Three Guinness and a Miller Lite," Henry told the bartender.

"My new BFF here, Mr. Henry Gereighty, is a newly recovering playwright," the lawyer said. "He's been free from the strings of a new play production for less than a day now so forgive him if he doesn't seem very well socialized. Our drinking is his process of reentering the land of the living."

"We're in a dive bar in the French Quarter of New Orleans in the middle of the night," the woman said. "Of course we're going to run into a derelict playwright. Tennessee Williams was a faggot and he lived in this town. Of course he was famous so he got away with it."

"Where are you people from?" Henry said.

"Charleston, South Carolina," the woman said. "Mt. Pleasant to be exact. It's where God lives."

"Do you think I could get his address from you? He and I need to talk. It's been a long time coming."

"Is there anymore Janis Joplin on the jukebox?" The boxer said.

"Good call," the lawyer said.

The lawyer lead the woman to the jukebox, and the fighter took Henry to the bar.

"Did you think there was going to be a brawl?" Henry said to the fighter.

"She's scrappy. And from the looks of you you're the same."

"Goddammit, am I that rough?" Henry said.

The fighter smiled and winked at Henry.

"I'll take that as meaning, 'yes you are but it's okay,'" Henry said.

"Are all gay derelict playwrights so sensitive about their looks?" The fighter said.

"What gay man isn't concerned with his looks? If gay men weren't vain the entire fitness industry would collapse. And who decided I'm derelict? I'm not derelict. Do you people even know what the word derelict means?"

"Ah, I see, it's the arrogance attached to a sense of superiority that gives off the derelict vibe."

"I'll accept arrogance. And I'll even accept the sense of superiority. If I didn't have those things I would have never gotten anywhere with my work."

"There; we have things in common after all," the fighter said. Then he took Henry's hands in his, "Let me see how you handle your life." He explored the scars and scabs. "Who do you fight?"

"Mostly brick walls."

"What did brick walls ever do to you?"

"They won't stop staring at me," Henry said.

"You're funny, too: a derelict New Orleans playwright comedian."

"Don't forget scrappy. I like the word scrappy, especially when it's describing me," Henry said.

"Okay then, you're scrappy, too."

"A toast to fighters," Henry said raising his glass.

The fighter raised his glass, too: "A toast to us."

"You're in much better shape than I am," Henry said.

"The difference between fighting people and fighting ideas," the fighter said.

"I'm no slacker," Henry said.

"No you're not," the fighter said.

Then, from the jukebox, the woman said, "Lets go swimming. I want to go swimming. God I love to go night swimming."

"Move this to the hotel?" The fighter said.

"Is there a bar?" The lawyer said.

"We'll have to stock up," the woman said. "I want to go swimming with my new BFF." Then she said to her husband, "Meet my new BFF."

"What say you, BFF?" Henry said to the lawyer. "Are we going to take this shit show on the road?"

"It doesn't sound like you have a choice," the fighter said to Henry.

"Are you going to be my BFF?" Henry said to the fighter.

Then the lawyer said, "We're all BFFs. All the world is my BFF. Then he said to the bartender, "Four two-finger pours of your best: two rum, two whiskey and make them for the road."

The bartender poured the drinks. The lawyer passed them out and said, "To the pool."

They were staying at a boutique hotel on Chartres Street a few blocks from the bar. It was a long, loud walk, though, as they veered from the path while struggling to harmonize to songs from the catalogue of Journey.

An hour later, halfway through the catalogue, they made it to the hotel. "I didn't realize we were staying so far away," the woman said.

"I believe we took the long way," the lawyer said. "Is it too late now?"

"For me," she said and kissed her husband and told her new friends goodbye and went upstairs.

There were cabanas down two sides of the pool. The fighter stripped to his jock, tossed his clothes into a cabana, and dived in. Henry, following suit, stripped to his briefs and did the same. Although Henry had a few years on the boxer he looked good without clothes on. The fighter's pecs and abs were chiseled, and the obliques showed shark bites. Henry liked to drink. The lawyer, having seen the two men strip, took off his shoes, rolled up his pants legs, sat on the edge of the pool and laid back. "You two have at it. I'm going to lay here and look at the stars and nurse this rum."

The men played in the water.

Then the fighter said, "You shouldn't be self-conscious about your looks. You look good."

"I appreciate that. Sometimes I think about juicing; nothing major, just enough to keep up. When you hit 40 it really does all change; that's not a myth."

"Don't. Aging isn't a bad thing. A man who takes care of himself, maintains his body though the aging process, is sexy as hell. That's what I want. It's kind of pathetic to see a 40 or 50 something man who looks plastic. My body at present is occupational. When I age out of fighting, this all goes away."

"The tragedy here is straight men actually seem to get that. Gay men don't. Gay men are more vicious. Gay men are probably the most homophobic group in the US. We're collectively a very narrow-minded bunch of folks."

"Don't juice. I would go for a guy like you. You would be my type," the fighter said then leaned over and kissed Henry. "I hope it's okay I did that. I've always wanted to do that; kiss a man."

"You can check it off your bucket list now?" Henry said.

"I can check it off my bucket list now. Have you always been...?"

"Yes," Henry said. "But I haven't always been out, if that's what you mean. I've always known. I've not always lived in places where it was okay, though. Like when I was growing up. A small southern, mountain town."

"So what do you do when it's like that?" The fighter said.

"You learn to keep your mouth shut, spend a lot of time staring at the floor to not have a wandering eye. And no one gets to know you."

"It sounds terrible," the fighter said.

"It was, and still is sometimes, depends on where you are," Henry said.

"Not in New Orleans, though," the fighter said.

"Well, the perimeters of acceptance are getting smaller with the population shift slash cultural upheaval," Henry said.

"Is that true?"

"It is factual," Henry said.

"So I came to New Orleans at a good time?" The fighter said.

"If you came to experiment I would say yes just because the acceptance level is changing. You should also know we've got the highest infection rate in the country. The product of an overtly homophobic state level government."

"That's a mood killer, isn't it?"

"Nah, it's become the standard precursor to foreplay," Henry said. "We just covered safe sex and my dick is still hard."

"So guys aren't really that different then at all: gay, straight and the plight of the hard dick?" With that the straight man stuck his hand under the water and grabbed Henry. "That's a hard dick."

"Consider it a compliment," Henry said.

"I do."

"Is it my turn to ask you stuff now?" Henry said.

"You can if you'd like," the fighter said.

"Will you be honest?" Henry said.

"Were you honest with me?"

"Brutally."

"Then I will be brutally honest with you," the fighter said.

"You seriously have never kissed another man?"

"No. Not until a few minutes ago," the fighter said.

"Are you gay?" Henry said.

"I think about it too much to not fess up to at least bi-," the fighter said. "I've ran ads in Craigslist before. I've never actually met anyone. Truthfully I've gotten off on the attention; on knowing I could get a guy."

"Being a gay guy isn't something you see as being tragic, is it?"

"No."

"It's not something you would hate about yourself, is it?" Henry said.

"No."

"Your wife?" Henry said.

"I don't know," the fighter said. "I'm beginning to reevaluate all the things I've always thought about love."

"Fair enough," Henry said.

"You were good timing," the fighter said then kissed Henry again.

Henry kissed him back this time.

The lawyer sat on the shallow end of the pool and sipped the rum and watched as the fighter climbed out of the water, took Henry's hand and pulled him out, too. Then he led Henry to a cabana and kissed him again. The fighter grabbed Henry's cock again and started to lower himself to his knees. Henry stopped him. "Are you sure about this?"

The fighter smiled his beautiful smile and said, "I'm sure. Is it okay with you?"

"Do I get to reciprocate?" Henry said.

"You're going to get to reciprocate."

The lawyer fumbled through his clothes to find a cigar and sat back in the pool. He lit the cigar and sipped the rum and watched as a meteor shower lit up the sky.

Just before the fighter slid inside Henry, Henry stopped him, *Oh shit, Frankie*, he thought.

He answered himself: Frankie's for fun. This body you've got your hands on is for fun.

*But there's an investment in Frankie.*

No there isn't. He made it clear. You made it clear.

*I'll tell him about it.*

Go ahead, it'll give him a good laugh and then he can tell you about all the guys he's fucked since you fucked him.

"Are you okay?" The fighter said.

"I want to take my time with you," Henry said.

Henry kissed him and in the kiss he dived into everything the man was and Henry was no more and the body he swam into was the world.

The process of sex with the fighter was necessarily slow, meticulous, and beautiful; a thousand soft kisses and hand-gliding, being fucked and fucking, forehead to forehead, and chest to chest to feel each other's breath and hair and skin. For the fighter this would be the high-water mark, the standard for all other encounters he would search out in a quest for love beyond the borders of cultural expectations. For Henry there was a bittersweet attachment as it was confirmation that Frankie was not forever.

"It's nice to know there are still some vestiges left of all the things this city used to be," Henry said to the lawyer as they made their way back towards the bar on Lower Decatur Street.

"What do you feel like?" The lawyer said.

"Guinness," Henry said.

"Breakfast?" The lawyer said.

"Too early yet. I'm not so sure I'm ready for this night to end."

"Then Guinness it shall be."

At the bar Henry excused himself to the pisser. The bathroom was in the courtyard down a long narrow hallway of exposed brick. He paced back and forth as he complained to himself: *I'm not so sure I'm ready for this night to end.*

Seriously, Henry? Is it a Prom date?

*I'm not so sure I'm ready for this night to end: stupid stupid thing to say.*

With that he punched the brick wall and bitched out loud: "What the fuck do you think this is? *Romeo and Juliet?*" He tried to shake off the pain, " 'I'm not so sure I'm ready for this night to end.' Stupid stupid fucking monkey."

Properly chastised, Henry went back to his stool at the bar. "You have a first-aid kit?" He said to the bartender, then turned to the lawyer, "I fell."

"Looks like a helluva fall," the lawyer said.

Henry doused his bloody knuckles with hydrogen peroxide and waited until the boiling stopped. Then he doused the bleeding places with rubbing alcohol, slapped on gauze, and taped it up.

"You must have done that before," the lawyer said.

"I'm a klutz," Henry said. "It comes with the territory."

The two switched to coffee because it was 4 am and they both had daytime things to tend to.

"I Googled you when you were out back," the lawyer said. "I didn't realize who you are."

"Tell me, please. I'd like to know."

"You're a real playwright, aren't you?" The lawyer said.

"Ex-playwright," Henry said.

They sat in silence, sipping the coffee till it cooled enough.

"Motherfuck," Henry said.

"Unicorn."

"I may have to puke before I drive back to the coast," Henry said.

"Do you drive the 90 back?" The lawyer said.

"Definitely."

"Then make yourself throw-up before you go. It's a little bouncy. Are you going to tell your boyfriend about...?"

"I don't have a boyfriend. Do you realize that my generation is the last generation to necessarily have the coming out story?"

"Do you do activism on the side or something?" The lawyer said.

"Isn't living with the audacity it takes to stand-up and be identified in itself an exercise in activism?"

"Oh yes, of course, so all gay men are necessarily activists then?"

"If only that were true. Can you even imagine an entire generation of homosexuals not navigating their childhoods in fear? I try to conceive it and I can't. It's more than I can wrap my head around."

"What do you think will come of the gay community in the midst of all this upcoming free thinking and freedom with the Millennials?" The lawyer said.

"Who knows. It's not much of a community as it is. Our community has always been defined by fear," Henry said. "Maybe that's why too many gay men treat other gay men as disposable."

"Fear is the single driving force behind all social phenomenon; both good and bad," the lawyer said. "Do you want to be just like the straight majority?"

"No. I don't care to blend in. I just think it's reasonable to not have to fear being authentic. Do you think polyamory is setting yourself up for a painful life? For loneliness at a core level?" Henry said.

"I think it could be the opposite," the lawyer said. "The goal is having love, not sacrificing the self."

"It seems lonely to me; never fully exposed to one man,"

Henry said. "I would think the bond of a relationship would be the trust in full exposure."

"That's flawed logic. Love is sacrifice, not consumption," the lawyer said as he started to laugh.

"What's so funny about it?" Henry said.

"We're wasting a lot of damaged brain power here on something that's fleeting at best. People don't react to Love. They react to Pain. If you want something out of someone you have to hurt them. Don't look so appalled. Love isn't clear, it confuses people. Pain is very clear, all of the time. Maybe guys who promote polyamory need to experience Pain on a fundamental level so they can then appreciate the defining opposition of Love. That's what I think about love and pain, for what it's worth. Go tell your boyfriend you fucked another guy and see if it hurts him. If it hurts him he's yours. If it doesn't you never had him to begin with. Sinner."

"Did you just call me a sinner? You're the lawyer, you're the sinner," Henry said then laughed. "Sinners."

The bartender brought in the morning paper. Henry and the lawyer divided it up and commenced to reading through it over coffee, sharing each section without words like an old married couple.

Henry and the lawyer stood outside Fiorella's watching the French Market come to life in first light as bickering vendors competed for the best spots.

"Run into you again sometime?" The lawyer said.

"I hope so," Henry said. "Thank you for listening to me. It was the best twenty bucks I ever spent."

As they walked off the lawyer stopped and said, "You realize you're going to be my first man crush."

"I should be so lucky," Henry said.

Then the two men went their separate ways, as the dark eased into the light and cast the first shadows of the day.

# 13

WHEN Henry got home he sat on the porch with a cup of soda water and Peychaud's bitters. After his stomach settled from the booze and Fiorella's grease he began to be hungry again and fried a pan of fish. He ate the tilapia with mustard potato salad from Winn Dixie. Then after eating he walked the two blocks to the beach and went swimming. Having food that he loved in his stomach made him feel good again. The noontime swim was the perfect close to the perfect night.

Later, with dried salt on his skin, hair matted with salt and sweat, he felt purged of the world as he worked on The Piss Map. He played the radio as he labeled a jar of piss and added it to the growing collection. Then added the name to the map. "I can't believe I forgot Bobby Jindal. You definitely get pissed on, my friend. Guilty of collusion with genocide I sentence you to a golden shower. Little Ronnie Reagan must be having wet dreams of you in his grave as you carry on his dubious legacy; what an asshole. You may very well get two jars." Then, on the wall labeled Those In Good Standing he added numbers 4 and 5: 4. Straight Lawyer from the bar whom I'm sure will be the best man at my wedding in the minute event that were to happen; and 5. Straight fuck in the cabana whom I'm sure would be in my life under better circumstances.

He stood back and looked at the new additions and scratched his head, "What's with all of these fucking straight people? Suddenly I'm a straight guy magnet."

He made another glass of the soda water and bitters and sat on the front porch swing. There was big band music on the radio that made him want to dance. He rocked himself in the porch swing, pushing back and forth with sunburnt bare feet, in tune to the Glenn Miller orchestra. At one point he could feel his heartbeat align with the music and he remembered the heart was a metronome. Since moving to the coast, since acquiescing to the erasure of his life as a New Orleans playwright, since discovering The Piss Map, his life started to become lighter and he began to feel a simple Happiness that he had lost in The Catastrophe. The music stopped and the news started and they talked about how the French Quarter community had been rocked again by another senseless murder. A local man, a lawyer was shot to death by two teenagers in a robbery in the early morning hours on the corner of Burgundy and Governor Nichols streets. The lawyer had been a long-time resident of the French Quarter. The young men, aged 15 and 17, were apprehended a few hours later breaking in to a neighborhood store on Marais Street in the Treme. Both young men wore court ordered ankle bracelets.

The Fuck You Wall grew a little more: Number 6. Kids Who Kill.

# 14

HENRY stopped at Hanks on St. Claude Avenue before meeting Frankie at the bar. He bought a couple of 12 packs of bottled beer and pulled into the old parking lot where Roberts grocery had been before the storm. The radio was playing salsa music. He turned it up as loud as it would go, and as he fell into the rhythm of the music he smashed the bottles against the wall. Mid-way through the bottles he could feel that ecstasy that comes with falling into the zone, losing yourself to something greater. Smashing the bottles became an ecstatic rush as he exorcised the anger; to such a degree that after the bottles were gone he threw the shards. When he had finished with that he sat on the hood of his car to catch his breath and bandage his hands where the shards had cut them open.

His throwing hand looked like a boxers, wrapped up in gauze and white medical tape red in all the places where bleeding was worse and soaked through.

Henry met Frankie at the bar where he worked. "You're pensive," Frankie said to Henry as he walked into the bar. "You're furrowed brow came through the door seconds before the rest of your head."

"I had an accident," Henry said.

"I hope the other guy looks worse."

"Okay then it wasn't that kind of an accident. It really wasn't an accident at all. By the way, I hate the word pensive," Henry said.

"I like learning the things you hate. It gives me ammunition. Are you in a pissy mood? If you're going to be pissy lets hang out another time. You're supposed to be for fun. You walk into the room and I want fun."

"I need fun. I'm a little pensive. I'm a little pissy. But I can shake those things and be fun for you."

"Let me see it," Frankie said taking Henry's bandaged hand. "I'm pretty sure this is an ER moment."

"No, it'll be fine," Henry said taking his hand back.

"I don't know, buddy," Frankie said.

"I hate the word buddy," Henry said. "'Buddy' suggests a child, or a trick. I am neither of those things. I was hurt earlier then I was angry and now I'm hurt again but it's a different hurt now."

"You're complicated."

"I'm not complicated."

"So that leads us back to pissy."

"And pissy leads to you not wanting to have fun with me, doesn't it?"

"Lets do this another time," Frankie said.

"No, no lets not. I'm sorry, I'll be fun. I really have been looking forward to seeing you. I was thinking on the way over here that I can't whistle. You should know that I can't whistle, Frankie; in the event that being a good whistler becomes a deal-breaker for you."

"So you're being funny now," Frankie said.

"I'm trying to turn it around and be fun for you," Henry said.

"If you're willing to try and do that then I'm willing to overlook some shortcomings like you not being able to whistle," Frankie said.

"Would you learn how to play the guitar for me?" Henry said.

"No," Frankie said.

"Would you be 'willing' to learn? It would be easier to move forward and be fun if you were at least willing to learn."

"My therapist told me I was a self-loathing homosexual. You're one, too, aren't you?" Frankie said. "You are. I can tell. Look at you. You're a mess. Who did you hit?"

"Is this the part of 'whatever it is we're doing' where you start parroting your therapist's observations as the cure-all of our relationship woes? And I didn't hit anybody, I was throwing glass."

"Every man our age is a self-loathing homosexual. It's what we were taught. Now somehow we've got to get beyond that so that we can love one another. I know about this kind of stuff, Henry. My mom agrees. My best friend agrees. My sponsor agrees. And this isn't a relationship. And why were you throwing glass?"

"You're in AA?" Henry said

"Not anymore. I quit."

"How's that working out for you?" Henry said.

"I'm a high-functioning alcoholic, everything is fine," Frankie said. "And you didn't answer my question."

"I was trying to stop hurting."

"Is the whole evening going to be cryptic? I'm not in the mood for cryptic. I'm being patient hoping things are about to turn around for the better."

"There was another murder in the Quarter this morning. Look, I promise I'm trying to not be morose and to be fun for you." With that, Henry leaned in to kiss Frankie on the cheek.

"What are you doing?" Frankie said.

"I'm going to kiss you if you'll stop moving. It's difficult to hit a moving target," Henry said.

"No you're not," Frankie said.

"You don't want me to kiss you?"

"Of course I do, just not here. Look over there, those people are watching us. Look at them. They're whispering to one another: 'Is he going to do it? Is he going to kiss him?'"

"Fuck them. Kiss me."

"No PDAs. You know that about me."

"I didn't agree to it," Henry said.

"You don't agree to someone elses PDA issues. You accept them or you don't. Which is it going to be?"

"I don't have plans to stand here in the middle of this bar and shove my tongue down your throat. It's a simple kiss. Straight people do it all the time."

"That doesn't mean I think it's a good idea."

"Okay, look, we're both in our 40s. You have baggage. I have baggage. My baggage isn't tragic. I was walking here trying to concentrate on how much my hand hurts so I wouldn't think about how much I was hurting inside and while I was doing that I started to think about the Williams' boys, and if Uncle Remus' bloodline is still alive in the south; because I like to think about those things, too, when everything else becomes too much to sort out. What do you think?"

"That's your baggage?"

"My baggage is lined with the melodramatic. It's a curse. I'm an ex-playwright. I drink whiskey and the right music comes on and a suitcase I forgot I had falls to the floor and flies open. The particular lining in this case has me worried about the loss of the Williams boys. They trouble me sometimes when I'm alone. You realize they charted the Southern landscape of Loneliness."

"The Williams' boys?"

"Hank and Tennessee."

"And Uncle Remus?"

"Compare Lapin; *Brer Rabbit.*"

"I forget you're a writer and then you remind me."

"You forget and I remind you. Are you saying I'm the real McCoy? My very language gives me away?"

"Let's talk about me now, Henry, and keep it light. I'm not into deep conversation tonight. I told you what you remind me of. Now you tell me what I remind you of. It'll be charming and then we can go back to my place and fuck. That is what I want from you tonight."

"I'm going to buy you a drink," Henry said. "I'm having a Compari and soda. It's a Compari and soda night. Lets have a drink then take a walk and you can tell me about your day. While you're telling me about all the things you did today I'll feel better because I'll feel less alone. Then maybe we can go back to the coast. There are a few bottles of the red left."

"Stay in the city with me," Frankie said.

"I want to wake-up to pancakes then walk on the beach. I want ownership," Henry said.

"I want to wake-up to bloody marys and a stroll to Croissant D'or and if I can't get that from you tonight I'll get I from somebody else."

"Is this about your whole polyamory theory?" Henry said. "If it is I'm pretty sure polyamory and being a whore are different things."

"It's about me not feeling like being a support system tonight," Frankie said.

"Last night I was exploring with the whole polyamory

thing myself and it wasn't me being a whore," Henry said. "Thirty-five, married, muscle, never been with a man before and was curious about the whole multiple intimate partner concepts, too; basically no single commitment just a network of friends with benefits. I fucked him by the pool at Le Richelieu."

"Why are you telling me that?" Frankie said.

"Because you said the whole thing interests you. I'm interested in you so I thought I'd experiment a little to see if maybe I could pull it off. I figured if I could pull that off then maybe I could have you long-term. I'd like to have you long-term. So I think I can do it."

"You're really vindictive, aren't you?" Frankie said.

"The sex was great."

"So you fuck someone else then come to me to listen to you bleat over a broken heart?" Frankie said.

"We're being polyamorous. Did you just say that I'm bleating? Do you think I'm a fucking sheep all of a sudden?" Henry said.

"Goddamn you, Henry. We agreed to be honest. If you want to fuck somebody else then fuck somebody else but tell me about it."

"I am. I just did," Henry said.

"Not after the fact as a casual missive. That's different. That's concealing information.. It's lying."

"You can't possibly be pissed off at me over that."

"I am pissed, Henry. And I'm done."

"Just like that?"

"Just like that," Frankie said. "This is drama. I didn't sign on for drama. It's simple."

Then Henry, forcing a smile, said, "Croissant D'or is fine with me. We can go to the coast next time. Here's something about me you didn't know: my favorite word is motherfuck."

"What the hell does that have to do with anything?" Frankie said.

"What's your favorite word? Let's change the subject and start again and do this better. What's your favorite word?"

"I don't have one. Why would I have a favorite word, Henry? What grown-ass man has a favorite word?"

"Motherfuck. I like the way it rolls out of my mouth. It's all-purpose, too: denigrating, incredulous, funny, angry. It may very well be the perfect word. Tell me that your favorite word is unicorn," Henry said.

"Whatever it is you're being right now? I don't like it."

"What I'm being is disappointed," Henry said.

"That's nice, very dramatic. The playwright in you is alive and well. Have a nice night, Henry," Frankie said. "I'm going home."

"I'll come with you. We can spend the night here and do all the things you want. Do you have any Hank Williams?"

"I don't have any Hank Williams and you're not coming with me."

Henry grabbed Frankie's hand. "Hold my hand, Frankie. We'll download some Hank Williams and fuck. Then in the morning we can get breakfast."

Frankie shook his hand loose. "Go home, Henry."

"You don't want to fuck to Hank Williams?" Henry said.

Frankie walked away.

Henry followed him outside and called after him, "You don't want to fuck to Hank Williams anymore, Frankie?"

Frankie moved from pool of light to pool of light before walking onto a dark block and disappearing.

Back on the coast Henry opened a bottle of the cheap red, climbed to the top of the ladder in the living room, and added Frankie St. Pierre to The Fuck You Wall.

# 15

IT'S easy to confuse consistency with love. Henry existed in that confusion where Frankie St. Pierre was concerned. A week had gone by since Frankie walked away. It was the first time since meeting that more than a day had passed without any communication. Whether it was missing a familiar body or missing an emotional bond was irrelevant because the end result was the same: The Missing.

In the living room, the name Frankie St. Pierre had been added to The Fuck You Wall three times, and scratched out each time.

Having scratched Frankie's name from the wall for the third time it was clear to Henry the status of Frankie St. Pierre had to be definitive. *What's it going to be, Frankie? You and me or nothing at all?* He bathed before driving into The City of NO. In the best of situations the trip would end with sex. In the worse he would return home with a new case of the cheap red.

Frankie was not at the bar. *He's shacking up with somebody,* Henry thought. He knew the statement that followed included himself but he held fast to the idea it was inherently true. Maybe the truth of it was another byproduct of the experiences of their generation, of being Children of Genocide, of living decades in hiding, of navigating their childhoods in Fear; perpetual inhabitants of The Land of Survival: Gay Men Instinctively Lie. Erase the Fear, erase the lie: maybe the Millennials will be able to pull it off. A flash of anger was immediately sent streaming through Henry's system. To his credit he recognized it for what it was. *There's no commitment here*, he thought. He stopped at Hanks and picked up a six pack of bottled beer. Then, because it was day, he headed over to the Bywater to smash them on the railroad tracks, pacing and talking to himself: " 'I'm a self-loathing homosexual,' Frankie said. 'You're one too. I can tell.' Fuck you, Frankie St. Pierre." The six pack was enough to calm him. He managed to quell the anger without bleeding.

He sat on the tracks and put his head in his hands, tears falling from his eyes onto the tops of his tanned southern feet and confided to no one: "What's wrong with me? What's wrong with me? What's wrong with me?"

Henry made his way to the Treme. Frankie St. Pierre lived in the middle of the block on Governor Nichols off Rampart Street. The building looked abandoned, even dilapidated; it's what made it such a find. Frankie's apartment was in the back and was one of two that were inhabited. The rest of the building sat empty and gutted; prime, wasted real estate – perhaps the only one of its kind left in the gentrified City of NO.

There was no front entrance to the building. A long concrete walkway lined the side and was closed off by a padlocked high fence. It took some doing but Henry climbed the fence. It wasn't a splashy high drama moment. He walked to the back of the building, climbed the flight of stairs, knocked on the door. No answer. Tried the knob.

The door opened. And Frankie was sandwiched between a couple of guys; fucking and getting fucked.

Back on the coast with a new case of cheap red Henry wrote definitively the name Frankie St. Pierre onto The Fuck You Wall. Then he went to the top of the wall marked Those In Good Standing and definitively scratched Frankie from the list. His anger wasn't satisfied with that. He moved the ladder to the opposite wall and added the name to The Piss Map. It was a solemn moment that he knew could never be taken back. Someone could be added to The Fuck You Wall and never make the progression onto The Piss Map as The Piss Map was application whereas The Fuck You Wall was consideration. There was no room for vacillation regarding those who made The Piss Map, ever.

Henry drank till he had to piss. He filled a Mason Jar, capped it, then labeled it:

> To be poured onto the grave of
>
> _____
>
> in the event I die before I have
> the opportunity to piss
> on their headstone in person

Then, with indelible ink, he filled in the blank with the name Frankie St. Pierre.

# 16

HENRY swam to release the anger. His hands hurt too badly to punch anything. "The saltwater will heal you up nicely," he told his hands.

After the swim he sat in the porch swing to sleep. "The sleeping will make you feel better," he told himself.

The first blow of the bat wasn't a solid hit. The Gimp misjudged the swing, otherwise it would have been a full-force blow to the head. It would have killed Henry instantly. The head of the bat smacked the wood swing and just enough of it made contact with Henry's ear to send a thunder clap through his dream. The impact, the sound, and the violent jerk of the swing sent him onto the concrete porch. Before he could get his bearings the Gimp made another swing, a better swing of the bat that caught Henry on the shoulder. The third swing was a solid impact to the ribcage that left Henry in the fetal position trying to protect himself.

Then there was silence. Then Henry could hear a woman's voice from somewhere close by. "Thaddeus? Come get your lunch, Thaddeus!"

Then Henry heard the bat fall and bounce on the concrete. As he relaxed Thaddeus kicked Henry in the face with the sole of his shoe, and then ran off the porch, down the railroad tracks, and into his own yard on the far side of the graveyard.

# 17

It was a long time before Henry sat up on the porch. Some of the lapse came from disbelief, some from pain, and some from having lost Frankie St. Pierre. "What's the problem, Henry?" He said to No One. "Don't you get off on this sort of thing? Aren't you the original Pain Junkie?"

"Fuck off," he answered himself.

Then he could hear The Actor: *If a playwright writes a new play and no one sees it did it ever exist to begin with? You missed the train.*

"What we did in this town matters," Henry said.

*Not anymore. If you want to make a comeback you're going to have to do it with* Naked Boys Singing, Part 2. *It's the only way, Henry.*

"I love this play."

*You have to reinvent yourself. You no longer have clout. It's as if you, me, none of us existed here to begin with. Nobody knows you or your work anymore, Henry. Its new population/new game. If you're going to survive you have to reinvent yourself.*

Henry and the last couple of bottles of the cheap red sat through the long night nursing his new wounds and making the definitive map for the Piss roadtrip. With a roll of newsprint he made a meticulous copy of The Piss Map; marking very specifically all the gravesites.

With first light he began to pack: a bag of clothes, his journal, the books that he loved, and all the jars of piss.

Packed, he cleaned out his bank account, took a marker and wrote on the outside of the front door of his house: Goddamn the following: Ronald Reagan, Jerry Falwell, the NIH, and the CDC, Selah. Then God, please damn: The New Population of The City of NO, 'Naked Boys Singing,' Frankie St. Pierre, and my rock throwing gimp of a neighbor Thaddeus. Amen.

He took the pirogue and his last play and walked to the beach. Fog moved slowly over the water and along the shoreline. It filled his lungs in a comforting way and he thought he no longer existed. It was beautiful to consider that his life was done and he had been granted amnesia of his demise so all he knew was the bliss of his feet in warm salt water and his head in the clouds, his lungs filled with the coolness that made his head light. It's enough to make you pity, he thought, those who still walk the earth without the sensations of being set loose, beaten by the usual sorrows of the world. It made him laugh. He stepped into the water that swirled around his feet, stretched out his arms, and said, "My steering current."

Henry placed the typewritten pages of a play called *Chapeau Tombe Nan La Mer* onto the seat of the little boat, then walked it into the Gulf of Mexico. When the water was waist high he pushed it as hard as he could.

The pirogue caught a steering current and was carried out to sea. A warm wind helped take the little boat and gently lifted the pages of the play up, page by page, and laid them on the surface of the waters, page by page, in order, as if for the gods to read.

Henry Gereighty watched the little boat disappear into the glare of the morning sun on the sea. Then he climbed into his car, and headed inland.

The gimp who wore a cape took the front door to Henry Gereighty's house from the hinges. He giggled to himself as he carried the door to the street for safety. Then he went back into Henry's house and set it on fire.

He replaced the front door of his own house with Henry's. And from that moment forth he never left his house without wearing lipstick, and he referred to himself as Mr. Henry from The City of NO.

# ABOUT THE AUTHOR

Louie Crowder's one act play, *A Better House for Ritchie*, was the 2013 winner of the Stonewall/Brickhouse Chapbook Competition, and was published by Stonewall/Brickhouse Books in Baltimore, Maryland, December 2013. It is available in paperback on Amazon.com, from the publisher, and from their distributor Itasca.

His first novella *In Irons*, published May 2014 by Gallatin & Toulouse Press in New Orleans, Louisiana, is available in both e-book and paperback on Amazon.com and from the publisher.

Follow Louie on Twitter, LinkedIn, Facebook, and at www.louiecrowder.com.